Disney's
A Winnie the Pooh First Reader

Bounce, Tigger, Bounce!

Adapted by Isabel Gaines

ILLUSTRATED BY Francesc Rigol

Disney PRESS

NEW YO

D1506588

First Edition

1 3 5 7 9 10 8 6 4 2

Library of Congress Catalog Card Number: 97-46693

ISBN: 0-7868-4255-5

For more Disney Press fun, visit www.DisneyBooks.com

Bounce, Tigger, Bounce!

Roo was waiting for Tigger.
He was beginning to think
Tigger would *never* come.

Just then, Tigger

bounced up the path.

He bounced so hard a big blob

of snow fell off the roof.

PLOP!

It landed on Roo's head.

7

"Hi, little buddy," Tigger said.

"Are you ready to go bouncing?"

"I am! I am!" Roo cried.

And off they went.

Tigger took big bounces, like this:

BOING! BOING! BOING!

Roo took little ones, like this:

BOING! BOING! BOING!

9

Tigger and Roo bounced
deeper into the woods.
Soon they came to a tall tree.
Roo looked way up
into the branches.

"Can Tiggers climb trees?"
he asked.

"Climbing trees is what Tiggers

do best," said Tigger.

"Only they don't just climb them.

They *bounce* them!

Here . . . I'll show you."

11

Tigger bent down, and Roo
hopped onto his shoulders.
Up the tree they bounced.
BOING! BOING! BOING!

Soon they reached

the very top.

Tigger looked down.

His head began to spin.

13

Suddenly, Tigger's tail

felt funny, too.

Roo was swinging

back and forth on it.

"S-s-stop that," Tigger begged.

"You're rocking the forest."

14

Just then,

Pooh and Piglet came by.

"HELP!" Tigger yelled down.

"Tigger!" Pooh yelled up.

"And Roo!

What are you doing up there?"

"Tigger is stuck," said Roo.

15

Pooh and Piglet hurried off
to get some help.
They came right back
with Kanga, Rabbit, and
Christopher Robin.

16

"Tigger is stuck," Roo

told his mother.

"That's too bad," she said.

"No, it's good," Rabbit said.

"Tigger can't bounce anyone

up there!"

"Well," said Christopher Robin,

"we have to get them *both* down."

17

Christopher Robin took off
his coat.
Pooh grabbed a corner.

18

"Here I come!" cried Roo.

"WHEEEE!"

He jumped right into the coat.

Then it was Tigger's turn.

"Jump, Tigger!" said
Christopher Robin.
"Tiggers don't jump,"
said Tigger. "They bounce."

"Then you'll have to climb down,"

said Christopher Robin.

"Tiggers *can't* climb down," said Tigger.

"Their tails get in the way."

And he wrapped his tail tightly

around the tree trunk.

"If I ever get down,"
Tigger gasped,
"I promise never
to bounce again!"
Rabbit's ears snapped
straight up.
"I heard that!" he cried.

Well, it took a while.

But not forever.

Tigger didn't jump down.

And he didn't climb down.

He just unwrapped his tail

and slo-o-owly slid down the tree.

PLOP!

Tigger landed in the soft snow.

He was so happy to be back

down, he felt like bouncing.

"No, no, no!" Rabbit cried.

"You promised. No bouncing!"

"You mean I can't *ever* bounce again?"

"Never," Rabbit said.

"Not even one teensy-weensy

bounce?" Tigger asked.

"Not even one," Rabbit replied.

Tigger's chin dropped.

His tail drooped.

Sadly he turned away.

Tigger's friends stared after him.

They all felt sad, too.

Except for Rabbit.

He was smiling.

27

Roo looked from Rabbit
to Tigger and back again.
"I like the old bouncy Tigger
best," he said at last.
"Me, too," everyone else said.
Everyone but Rabbit.

"What about you, Rabbit?"

said Kanga.

"Well," said Rabbit. "I . . . ah . . .

I . . . that is, I . . ."

For once, Rabbit didn't know

what to say.

29

Rabbit thought about all
the times Tigger had bounced him.
Then he thought about how sad
Tigger seemed without his bounce.
"Oh, all right," he finally said.
"I guess I like the old Tigger
better, too."

Before Rabbit could change
his mind, Tigger said,
"Come on, Rabbit.
Let's you and me bounce."

"Me bounce?" Rabbit said.

"Why not?" Tigger said.

"You have the feet for it."

Rabbit looked down

at his big, flat feet.

"I have?" he said.

"You have!" everyone

else agreed.

Rabbit tried a little bounce.

BOING!

Then he tried a bigger one.

BOING!

Soon he was bouncing

just like Tigger.

33

"Come on," Rabbit cried.

"Everybody bounce!"

And so they did.

They all bounced

together through

the Hundred-Acre Wood!

Join the Pooh Friendship Club!

A wonder-filled year of friendly activities and interactive fun for your child!

The fun starts with:

- Clubhouse play kit
- Exclusive club T-shirt
- The first issue of "Pooh News"
- Toys, stickers and gifts from Pooh

The fun goes on with:

- Quarterly issues of "Pooh News" each with special surprises
- Birthday and Friendship Day cards from Pooh
- And more!

Join now and also get a colorful, collectible Pooh art print

Yearly membership costs just $25 plus 15 Hunny Pot Points. (Look for Hunny Pot Points 3 on Pooh products.)

To join, send check or money order and Hunny Pot Points to:

Pooh Friendship Club
P.O. Box 1723
Minneapolis, MN 55440-1723

Please include the following information: Parent name, child name, complete address, phone number, sex (M/F), child's birthday, and child's T-shirt size (S, M, L)
(CA and MN residents add applicable sales tax.)

Call toll-free for more information
1-888-FRNDCLB

Fun for kids ages 3-8!

Help your child learn MATH and READING with a computer and a silly old bear.

©Disney

Disney's Learning Series on CD-ROM

Put your child on the path to success in the 100 Acre Wood, where Pooh and his friends make learning math and reading fun. Disney's Ready for Math with Pooh helps kids learn all the important basics, including patterns, sequencing, counting, and beginning addition & subtraction. In Disney's Ready to Read with Pooh, kids learn all the fundamentals including the alphabet, phonics, and spelling simple words. Filled with engaging activities and rich learning environments, the 100 Acre Wood is a delightful world for your child to explore over and over. Discover the magic of learning with Pooh.

Once Again The Magic Of Disney Begins With a Mouse

Wonderfully Whimsical Ways To Bring Winnie The Pooh Into Your Child's Life.

Pooh FRIENDSHIP

Pooh and the gang help children learn about liking each other for who they are in 5 charming volumes about what it means to be a friend.

Pooh STORYBOOK CLASSICS

These 4 enchanting volumes let you share the original A.A. Milne stories — first shown in theaters — you so fondly remember from your own childhood.

Pooh PLAYTIME

Children can't help but play and pretend with Pooh and his friends in 5 playful volumes that celebrate the joys of being young.

Pooh LEARNING

Pooh and his pals help children discover sharing and caring in 5 loving volumes about growing up.

FREE*
Flash Cards Attached!
A Different Set With Each
Pooh Learning Video!
* With purchase, while supplies last.